PATCH & MARY

A SAMC Christmas to Remember

STEEL ARCHANGELS BOOK 3.5

R. KNIGHT

Title: Patch & Mary: A SAMC Christmas to Remember (SAFC3.5)

Series: Steel Archangel's MC (Book 3.5)

Copyright 2024 R. Knight Publications LLC

Paperback Copyright 2025 R. Knight Publications LLC

All rights reserved.

Cover by: JG Designs

Formatting by: Becky Hodges

Edited by: Franklin Beck

Contents

Dedication	V
Acknowledgements	VI
Reading Order & Other Works By R. Knight	VII
Content & Trigger Warning	IX
Steel Archangels MC Members Forest Creek Chapter (SAFC)	X
Steel Archangels MC Members Junction Creek Chapter (SAJC)	XII
Translation Glossary	XIII
Song Inspiration	XV
Synopsis	XVI
1. Chapter 1 Patch	1
2. Chapter 2 Mary	6
3. Chapter 3 Patch	13
4. Chapter 4 Cassie	18
5. Chapter 5 Ash	21

6. Chapter 6   25
    Izzy

7. Chapter 7   30
    Patch

8. Chapter 8   35
    Patch

9. Chapter 9   41
    Mary

10. Chapter 10   47
    Mary

11. A Biker's Prayer   54

12. Author's Note   55

13. About the Author   56

Dedication

To MY LOVING HUSBAND and children. Your continued support means the world to me. Thank you for being there for me through thick and thin, and for listening to my crazy ideas ;) <3

To those of you that fell in love with Patch, Mary, and their kids, I hope you enjoy their first Christmas together as a family and with the club <3

Acknowledgements

To MY READERS, THANK you for joining me as the Steel Archangel's MC celebrates Christmas <3 You're continued support means the world to me!

Becky, my fantabulous PA, thank you for spurring me on to write this! I was toying with the idea but wasn't sure if I should do it as a novella or tie it in with Reaper's story. Thank you for the push <3 Love you!

To my Alpha Team, you guys really rock! I hit you guys hard this month with two books and you all came through for me <3 Thank you for your support and being there for me when I needed to bounce ideas around and so much more! Love you all <3

To my editor, formatter, and cover designer, thank you all for everything you did to help make this book what it is! I love working with all of you <3

Reading Order & Other Works By R. Knight

Steel Archangel's MC

Thor & Dragon (SAFC1)
Timber (SAFC2)
Patch (SAFC3)
Patch & Mary: A SAMC Christmas to Remember (SAFC3.5)
Reaper (SAJC1—coming soon)
Smoke (SAFC4—TBD)
Cannon & Atlas (SAJC2—TBD)

Children of Prophecy

Hell's Lost Princess, Book 1
Book 2 (coming soon)

<u>Shifter Royalty</u>

Mates, Book 1

Spirits, Book 2

Book 3 (coming soon)

<u>Standalones</u>

New Beginnings

*This is in the process of being rewritten
and rebranded. The link will be coming soon*

Content & Trigger Warning

THIS BOOK IS INTENDED *for a mature audience aged 18+. It contains foul language and adult situations.*

Each book can be read as a standalone, but it is best read in order as the story builds on the members and their women/partners in the Steel Archangel's MC.

Steel Archangels MC Members

Forest Creek Chapter (SAFC)

Ryan Gilbert (Thor)—President

Reed Thomson (Phoenix)—Vice President

Nick Gilbert (Dragon)—Enforcer

Alexander 'Alex' Carter (Ryder)—Sergeant at Arms

Elijah Anderson (Tripp)—Secretary

Liam Caldwell (Timber)—Treasurer

Noah Banks (Judge)—Road Captain

Levi Gilbert* (First Lady)—Unofficial 2nd Enforcer

Jaxon 'Jax' Witlock (Smoke)

Luke Morgan (Patch)

Malcolm Hart (Bones)

Michael Adams (Gunner)

Aiden Hunt (Axe)

Owen Burke (Bear)

Troy Simpson (Cowboy)

Drae Black—Prospect

Alexei Petrov—Prospect [pronounced ALEX-AY]

Sasha Petrov—Prospect [pronounced SAWSHA]

Ethan Mills—Prospect

Old Ladies

Levi Gilbert*—Old Lady to Thor & Dragon
Mae Caldwell—Old Lady to Timber
Mary Catarino—Old Lady to Patch

Children

Lindsey Joy Black—Daughter to Drae Black
Asher 'Ash' Morgan—Son to Patch & Mary
Isaiah 'Izzy' Hayes—Son to Patch & Mary
Cassandra 'Cassie' Hayes—Daughter to Patch & Mary

Steel Archangels MC Members

Junction Creek Chapter (SAJC)

Anthony 'Tony' Leyton (Reaper)—President

Isaac Lopez (Devil)—Vice President

Kai Miller (Punisher)—Enforcer

Leon Foster (Razor)—Sergeant at Arms

Tyson Manning (Smithy)—Treasurer

Grant McGee (Beast)—Secretary

Adam Collins (Loki)—Road Captain

Cole Thornton (Python)

Hunter Beck (Doc)

Ragnar Miller (Odin)

Duncan Goodwin (Atlas)

Theodore 'Theo' Harris (Cannon)

Drake Olsen—Prospect

Nathan Flynn—Prospect

Old Lady

Astrid Miller—Old Lady to Odin

Translation Glossary

BELOW YOU WILL FIND the glossary list for the translations that will appear in *Steel Archangel's MC: Patch & Mary: A SAMC Christmas to Remember*.

The Greek translations below include the declension cases (nominative, genitive, accusative, and vocative or the masculine, feminine, and neuter nouns) and they will be seen in the body of each chapter since the Greek words will alter slightly depending on how they are being used in a sentence. As with the previous books in the *Steel Archangel's MC* series, translations will appear for the first four times in each chapter.

Please note that a word could have the same ending for more than one declension case in the Greek language. For example (see below), 'mom' and 'moms' for the female nominative, accusative, and vocative cases have the '$α$' ending but the female genitive case has the '$ας$' ending. Same for 'dad' and 'dads' where the '$ας$' ending is for the masculine nominative case, whereas the '$α$' ending is for the masculine genitive, accusative, and the vocative cases. Also, the words like 'mom' and 'dad' are not capitalized in the Greek language, so you will not see them capitalized here.

Greek Word

Μαμά / μαμά (mama = mom)
Πατέρας / πατέρας (pateras = father/dad)
Ἄγγελος / ἄγγελος (aggelos = angel)

Declension Cases (Singular)

Song Inspiration

Here Comes Santa Claus by Gene Autry
Rudolph the Red Nose Reindeer by Gene Autry
Frosty the Snowman by Billy Idol
Jingle Bell Rock by Bobby Helms
I Saw Mommy Kissing Santa Claus by Jackson 5

Synopsis

IT'S OUR FIRST HOLIDAY together as a family, and as a bonus, it's Christmas—Mary's favorite holiday. Our kids have never been able to fully celebrate a holiday, ever, and I plan to change that. I'm going to give our kids and Mary a Christmas to remember.

To make things even more perfect, the entire club gets into the festive spirit and vows to give their new family members a Christmas they won't forget. A certain club member takes it even further and dons a big red suit to surprise the kids. Can you guess who? ;) :)

Join Patch and the Steel Archangel's MC as they plan a Christmas to remember.

Chapter 1
Patch

"Ooooof," the air whooshes out of me as a weight lands heavily on my stomach and an adorable giggle permeates through the haze of sleep. Cracking open my eyes, I'm not surprised to see my adorable baby girl straddling my stomach, her little hands covering her mouth in an attempt to keep her giggles quiet but failing terribly. Turning my head to look at my clock on the nightstand, I groan internally when I realize it's 6 am. Cassie's normally an early riser, but even this is too early for her.

"Good morning, ἀγγελε (angel)."

She giggles happily again at me using the Greek word for her nickname, Angel. A few days ago, after I proposed to Mary in what will be her restaurant, the kids had asked to start learning Greek and Spanish, which of course, had both of Mary's families beyond ecstatic. So, for the past couple of days, we've slowly been teaching the kids small words and phrases to start with. For now, it's just angel and Mom that they've learned.

We've tried teaching them the Greek word for dad, πατέρας (dad), but they have problems pronouncing it correctly most of the time. Then, I damn near came close to crying when Cassie told me that since most people don't know Greek, she's happy to call me 'Daddy' for a while longer yet so that everyone will know I'm her daddy. When the boys agreed with her, I'd hugged them close after that, feeling like my heart was going to burst out of my chest with love for all of them.

It's been a few days since we took care of Mary's demons, but the kids seemed to have blossomed overnight. We still haven't told them Stephan is dead, but somehow, they just seem lighter. It's almost as if they can sense he's no longer a threat to them.

"Morning, Daddy! It's Christmas Eve!"

As sleep releases its clutches on me, I smile. I love hearing *all* my kids calling me 'Daddy'. Smoke's already changed Ash's name back to Morgan since I am biologically his father. Someday, hopefully soon, Cassie and Isaiah will have my last name as well, and I can't wait. I have something special for them planned when Mary and I get married early next year. Hopefully they'll like it.

"That it is. Are you excited for Santa to come tonight?"

The kids have been having a blast with everything we've done the last few days with decorating all of the exteriors of the houses on the clubhouse grounds as well as the exteriors of the condos. We even decked out the guard shacks at the gate. We purposefully saved the clubhouse for last, though we did let the kids help decorate the outside of it two days ago. That's another thing that I love about my brothers and sisters. They know the importance of the kids finally being able to celebrate. To *really* celebrate a holiday. They went all in on everything and included Mary and the kids in every step.

Cassie's little head bobs up and down so quickly, I can't help but chuckle. Mary rouses next to me and I look over at her as she slowly blinks and takes us in. A soft smile spreads across her face when she sees that Cassie has, once again, woken me up like this and she shifts so that she's resting her head on my shoulder. Leaning down slightly, I press a kiss to the crown of her head.

"Good morning, ἀγγελε (angel)," Mary tells her and I bite my lip to keep in a groan of pain when Cassie hops up and down again on my stomach in excitement, landing hard each time.

"It's Christmas Eve, μαμά (mom)! Santa's going to come tonight!" Cassie shouts excitedly, and my hands quickly grab her around her little waist to prevent her from knocking the air out of me again. Mary chuckles, her voice husky from sleep and if our daughter wasn't currently in our room, I'd be making other plans.

"That it is," Mary says before looking up at me, her eyes sparkling.

Much like the kids, there's a weight that's been lifted off Mary's shoulders after we dealt with her demons. While she still has occasional nightmares and moments where she questions herself because of how Stephan had 'trained' her, the episodes have greatly decreased with her ending both Stephan and her mother by her own hands. So far, she hasn't had any nightmares relating around ending two lives with her own hands, but if she ever does, I'll be here for her.

"Can we make cookies for Santa and the reindeer?"

Mary nods and then pauses as she turns her attention back to Cassie. "We can make them for Santa, but the reindeer can't eat cookies. We'll have to make something different for them."

Cassie practically vibrates with excitement as she cheers and both Mary and I shush her as we try to stifle our own laughter.

"Quiet, άγγελε (angel), you don't want to wake your brothers," I chide and Cassie's eyes take on a glint of mischief. Mischief that I'm happy to see because she knows she's allowed to be a *real* kid with me. All of them are. Yes, they do still get in trouble every now and then, but even then, I'm proud of them because they have been starting to realize we really do mean what we say. Will they get in trouble if something gets broken? Yes. Will they get hurt? Hell fucking no.

I groan, playing along. "Did you already wake your brothers, άγγελε (angel)?" I tease her and she giggles again as she nods her head.

"I jumped on my knees on Izzy's bed and then we both jumped on Ash's bed! They're downstairs playing the racing game."

I'm glad she specifies they were on their knees because all three of them got in trouble the other day for literally jumping on their beds.

Cassie pouts a little at that last part because she isn't very good at playing video games just yet. Though I will give her brothers credit that they always let her play when she wants to, and they encourage her throughout the race. When she doesn't understand or know how to do something, they teach her what controls do what and how to do the tricks. No matter how many times they have to repeat themselves, they never let any frustration show. Those boys will do anything for their little sister.

I pick her up, holding her above me, almost like you'd hold a kid when they wanted to play 'airplane', and she shrieks with laughter. I wiggle my fingers slightly, tickling her sides, and her shrieks and giggles intensifies.

After a few moments, I set her down on the bed in between us.

"Go get changed, ἀγγελε, and brush your teeth. I'll do your hair after I get ready," Mary tells her and I wince when Cassie loudly shrieks again in excitement before she climbs off our bed and then races out into the hall.

"We get to make cookies for Santa!" she yells out and I hear the boys excited cheers in response.

Leaning forward, I place a far too chaste of a kiss on my Siren's lips, but the kids are waiting. I won't make them wait on a day like today.

"Let's get ready, Siren, and you can put me to work."

She grins widely, but I don't say anything about the relief I see on her face as well. It will take time, but I'll show Mary through my actions and words that I'm here for everything. Even if it means I'll be covered in flour and sprinkles.

Mary throws off the covers, shimmying to the side of the bed until she can get to the little scooter that Doc had shipped to us. It's one that you can kneel on the padded seat and then scoot around. She absolutely loves it and I know it's because she's regained some of her freedoms for moving around. There are still a few more weeks left that Mary has to wear the cast on her leg, but her shoulder has healed up enough to where she doesn't need to use the sling anymore. She still has a way to go before she regains her full strength back in her shoulder, but I know she'll get there in time.

Getting out of bed, I grab some clean boxers out of the dresser and cross the room. Walking into the bathroom, my cock immediately hardens at seeing Mary getting undressed. I strip quickly and grip the base of my cock hard, willing it to go down. I must make a sound because Mary looks over her shoulder at me and her eyes darken with lust when she looks down at my cock, which does nothing to help deflate my hard on.

"Later, Siren." Stepping forward, I kiss her. "I don't want to keep the kiddos waiting. Not today."

Her face softens and she leans up and kisses me again. "Thank you," she whispers.

Cupping her cheek, I shake my head. "You don't have to thank me for this. I love spending this time with our kids and seeing their eyes light up at all the decorations or whatever else we're doing. It's an honor to be a part of this with them and I know the others feel the same way. We'll give them a Christmas to remember. Our first Christmas as a family."

Her eyes turn misty, and I pull her into my arms, holding her. After a few moments, she pulls away and wipes her eyes.

"It means so much to me that you and the club are doing this for them, for me. Christmas has always been my favorite holiday, and I've missed all the decorating, the treats, just... everything. I know I don't have to thank you or the others, but still, thank you because this means the world to us."

For a moment, my anger rises at everything Mary and the kids have missed out on, but I immediately squash it. It will take time before it fully sinks in that she has her freedom back, but until then, I'll be here to keep reminding her and supporting her.

Giving her another kiss, I reach around her and turn on the shower before looking back down and winking at her. "Well, then, let's get your leg wrapped, get ready, and get you in the kitchen because I know you've been itching to get back in there."

The blinding smile she gives me has my chest warming. Today's going to plan so far, minus being woken up a few hours early, but I have a feeling today will be one that we'll all remember, and not just the five of us.

Chapter 2
Mary

LEANING AGAINST THE KITCHEN cabinets, I pause as I look around the kitchen at my kids and Luke and I smile. Sure, the counters may be covered in flour, frosting and chocolate smears, and sprinkles. The kids, and even Luke and I, are covered in flour. The sink is filled with dishes that need to be washed. There are trays littered across our counters and the table with cookies cooling and waiting to be decorated, as well as tons of containers full of cookies that have already been decorated. More cookie dough is waiting in the fridge, ready to be rolled out and cut out. But you know what?

I wouldn't change a thing.

Seeing my kids laughing and smiling like this heals a crack in my battered heart. A heart that Luke is working so hard to help mend.

My smile widens as Cassie holds up two bottles of sprinkles and asks Luke and the boys for their opinion on what color she should use for the nose on her reindeer cookie. I'm relieved, though I shouldn't have been surprised, that Luke takes her question seriously instead of just brushing it off. I knew the boys wouldn't brush her off, as they adore Cassie to bits, but this is just one more example of how great a man Luke really is.

"Well, which one do *you* think would be better for the reindeer nose?" Luke asks her and her little face scrunches up as she debates whether to use the red or the pink sprinkles.

"I don't know. I can't choose. They both look so pretty." Her little face falls and I see tears starting to well in her eyes.

Just as I'm about to step, well scoot, forward, Luke reaches across the island. With his finger, he lifts her chin so she's looking at him, and his thumb brushes away a tear that falls.

Seeing her tears has me wishing I had made Stephan suffer more, but frankly, I'm just glad the asshole is gone. Now all that's left is to try and break the invisible shackles we all still wear and to get over the nightmares.

"Ἄγγελε (Angel), if you want to use both, then we'll use both. Heck, we could even use all the colors and make their noses sparkle like a rainbow."

"Really?" Izzy asks, his face lit up with hopeful excitement.

"Yup," Luke says, smiling widely at them as he rubs his hands together. "Rainbow reindeer cookies it is!"

Turning, I open the cupboard and dig around, looking to see if I have anything else they can use.

As I do, I hear Luke taking another picture. He's been snapping pictures left and right this morning. Then again, I'm guilty of doing the same.

Reaching inside the cupboard, I pull out a few other Christmas cookie cutters. Some of them are duplicates of what I already have out, but it sounds like we'll need them. I have a feeling we'll be baking up even more of a storm today than we already have. Hell, we'll probably be eating cookies for weeks. Well, maybe one week with how much the guys can eat. I pause when I see the extra sprinkles and toppings I'd held back earlier so that we didn't use everything at once, and debate if I should just pull it all down. Some of them aren't Christmas related, but I don't really think the kids will care. The sound of more giggles makes up my mind and I grab everything, arranging them on the counter.

"Oh, kids, μαμά (mom) pulled out the big guns!" Luke says and the kids' excited voices get even louder.

I bring the sprinkles and toppings they don't already have over to the island and the couple bags of cookie cutters. Leaning down, I boop Cassie on the nose and am rewarded with her adorable giggle and another bright smile. "Well, rainbow reindeer were requested, so that's what we're going to make happen." Pausing, I lift the bag of frosting, twisting the end to push more frosting toward the tip and then look at each of my kids. "Now, whose turn was it to help me put on the frosting?"

A knock on the front door has me looking in that direction. I can tell it's one of the club members, but due to the design in the glass part of the door, I can't tell who it is.

Turning toward Luke, I tilt my head in the direction of the door. "Could you get that?" I'm helping Ash put the frosting on his batch of cookies and I don't really want to stop right now.

Luke smiles and leans down, wiping off some frosting I somehow got on my cheek, and then licks it off his finger. My thighs clench at the action and I mock glare at him. He smirks and winks at me before leaning down to kiss me. It ends way too quickly for my liking. That said, I'm looking forward to tonight when the kids go to bed. Patch doesn't think I know about his not so little secret, but he doesn't know that I have one of my own. While he's taking care of his secret, I'll get ready with mine.

Luke grabs a towel off the counter and wipes his hands as he walks into the living room toward the front door.

Looking back down, I push down my lusty thoughts for now and continue helping Ash decorate his cookies. A moment later, I hear two deep, hushed voices talking and I try to ignore them. I'm sure it's something about our Christmas plans, but in case it's club business, I don't want to eavesdrop.

A few moments later, I hear Phoenix's loud laughter and look up to see him and Luke coming into the kitchen. I pause at his hesitant smile, but it relaxes some as he sees the mountains of cookies we've finished, the ones we're currently working on, and the giant ball of dough we still need to roll out.

"Looks like you've all had a fun morning," he says and then reaches out to ruffle Izzy's hair as he's closest to him. His eyes once again turn hesitant when he looks over at me. "Could I talk to you for a sec, Mary?"

Nodding, I bite my lip in worry. Is something wrong? Phoenix is the Vice President of the club. Have things gotten too out of hand? Do we need to do something different?

"It's okay, Siren," Luke whispers in my ear as he wraps one arm around my waist and with the other he takes the frosting bag out of my hands. "Nothing's wrong, he just wants to chat. I'll continue to help the kids. Why don't you go into our room to talk so you guys can have some privacy?"

Swallowing thickly, I nod again. "Okay. Let me just wash my hands."

I don't look up at Phoenix as I back away from the counter and scoot over to the sink to wash my hands. After drying them, I take off my apron and dust as much of the flour off my clothes as possible. When I'm done, I still don't look at Phoenix as I cross the room with my scooter. After finally finding peace, for the most part, a part of me is still waiting for the other shoe to drop. Is this when it drops? But then again, Luke wouldn't leave me alone with Phoenix if he didn't trust him. Especially alone in our room.

I jump slightly when the door clicks shut behind us and I wheel over to the bed and sit down on it.

"Please stop thinking those thoughts." The pain in Phoenix's voice has my head snapping up and I suck in a breath at seeing the pain etched on his face and in his eyes as well. "You aren't in trouble or anything and we aren't kicking you out. Same for the kids. I just..." He pauses as he sheepishly scratches the back of his neck. "I just... Fuck, I'm not good at this shit."

Heaving a heavy sigh, he turns, stalks across the room to the armchair and then picks it up, which I'm thankful for because I don't want the hardwood floors in here to get scuffed. Especially since the club owns these condos. He carries the armchair over so that it's in front of me before he sinks heavily into the cushions.

"I've been battling with myself ever since you helped patch me up from that explosion earlier this month."

He's silent for a bit after that and I force myself to swallow around the lump in my throat. "Why were you battling with yourself?"

His shoulders slump even more and he rests his elbows on his legs as he stares down at his hands. "Because I wanted to claim you as my sister, but I thought I'd be disrespecting my own sister's memory."

I inhale sharply. Did his sister die? He nods at my unspoken question. Crap... Did I say that out loud again?

"What happened to her?" my voice is shaky, and I'm almost too scared to ask, but it's obviously something that's weighing heavily on him.

His eyes go distant and the pain in them would have made my knees buckle if I had been standing. I curse myself internally for pushing him. Maybe he isn't ready to talk about it.

Phoenix shakes his head slightly. "I didn't have the best home life as a kid. My dad was an alcoholic. For the most part, he just drank until he passed out. Sometimes he'd get angry, and Ma would tell me to take Ember, my little sister, to our room. However, the paper thin walls did nothing to hide the sounds of him hitting her. Most of the time we got to our room without him catching us, but sometimes we weren't as lucky. I tried to take the brunt of it for Ember, telling her to run and hide. Even with everything he did to her and us, Ma still stood by him. He had his claws so deep in her that she'd never leave him. Well, has, I should say. Even with him in prison, I know she still stands by him from what I've heard."

He pauses and his eyes take on an even more pained edge.

"When I was eight and Ember was six, we were quietly playing outside in the backyard when Dad came barreling out of the house at us, yelling at us for being too loud and waking him up." He pauses and scrubs his hand over his face. "We both tried to tell him it wasn't us that was making the noise, but he wouldn't listen. He backhanded me so hard that I fell to the ground and was seeing stars. When I looked up, I saw Dad shaking Ember back and forth like a rag doll and hitting her face as he continued to yell at her. I shot to my feet and tried to get her out of his clutches."

His hands fist in anger and his face hardens.

"I couldn't though. He was too strong and I was only eight. Still, I tried to claw his hands off her, even if it did earn me more hits. At that point, his yelling drew the attention of the neighbor kids who were outside playing and they yelled for their parents. Cops were called, but it was too late. Right as the cops arrived, he tossed Ember to the ground and her head hit the pavement with a sickening thud and then tried to go after me. In the end, the cops had to stun him to get him cuffed and stuffed in the back of their cruiser.

"Ember was rushed to the hospital but she died before they even got there. Dad got forty years in jail for killing her, but Ma still stayed by his side, even during the trial. She tried to paint me as a liar but the neighbor kids and their parents saw enough to convince the judge that what I was saying was true. After that, Ma did only what she needed to do to keep me alive.

"Ma blamed me for Ember's death saying I knew better and should have kept her quiet. She still didn't believe me that it was the neighbor kids that were the ones making all the noise that woke Dad up. She also hated me for putting him in jail and never let me forget that I was the cause of 'all her problems' as she put it. That she now had to work instead of relying on Dad to take care of the bills.

"Most of the time, I was left home alone with hardly any food and I was forbidden to touch the thermostat. In the winter, Ma kept the house just warm enough that the pipes wouldn't burst, and in the summer, I wasn't allowed to turn on the air conditioner. My clothes were worn until they were thread bare and when I needed new clothes, she would only take me to thrift stores. The only things I got brand new were socks and underwear.

"Whenever Ma was home, I became her verbal and physical punching bag that she used to vent her frustrations on. If it wasn't for Poseidon and Marie, Thor and Dragon's parents, I would have starved or froze to death if she didn't kill me herself first. When they saw what Ma was doing to me, they stepped in and took me in. I still don't know what Poseidon said to Ma to make her agree to let me live with them, but it worked. After that, the only times I saw her was around town, but she never approached me nor I her. She's dead to me. Her and Dad both. If she could have been stronger, maybe we could have gotten away from him sooner and Ember would still be alive."

"Oh, Phoenix."

He continues to stare out the window, blinking rapidly as if to keep tears at bay. Shifting, I stand on my good leg and then sit on my scooter so that I'm right in front of him, our knees almost touching. I take his rough, calloused hands in mine and squeeze them.

"I'm so sorry."

His hands tighten around mine and he turns back toward me.

"I finally realized, after talking with Punisher, that Ember wouldn't mind me claiming you as my sister." His face softens a bit, but it's still etched in pain. "You remind me so much of her, which is another reason why I was struggling. I didn't want you to think I was claiming you because of that. I wanted to claim you because I see you as family. My family. I knew it that day when you put me in my place and told me to can it. That you were going to be Doc's second set of hands whether I liked it or not." His shoulders slump again and an almost dejected look comes over him. "I'm sorry it took me so long to straighten out my shit."

I frown. "Don't talk like that."

He looks up at my tone and I realize I must have snapped more than I meant to. I give his hands another reassuring squeeze.

"Don't belittle your feelings. They're important. I would hate it if you claimed me and then later regretted doing so. I'd love to have you as an older brother, but only if that's something you really want. If you do want to claim me, know that I have no intention of taking Ember's place but would love to honor her memory with you, if that's something you'd be okay with?"

He stares at me, an emotion I can't quite place in his eyes. Then the next thing I know, I'm in his arms as he lifts me off the scooter and sets me down on his lap, hugging me to his chest. I wrap my arms around him, hugging him back. He kisses the crown of my head before tucking it under his chin.

"You're mine now, Sis."

My arms tighten around him. "And you're mine."

After a few moments, I pull back. "Do you still want me to call you Phoenix?" Surprisingly, he nods.

"After everything that happened, I hated the name my parents gave me which was Reed. When I prospected, Poseidon asked me if I had any ideas about what I wanted for a road name, which was a bit odd since normally you don't get to pick your road name. However, those that were in the military sometimes request to keep the monikers they earned while serving. I told him Phoenix. Ember used to love fairy tales and fantasy books. She always said if she could be something else, she'd be a phoenix. I was shocked that he let me have that as a road name, but he also knew how much Ember meant to me."

Blinking away my tears, I swallow thickly. "Then Phoenix it is."

Chapter 3
Patch

As Mary and Phoenix come out of our room after their talk, I cock an eyebrow in question at him. When he arrived, he told me about his intentions, and I was all for it. Personally, I think they both need each other.

Ever since the explosion earlier this month, I've noticed Phoenix has been a bit off. Something was bothering him, and I suspected it was because of his sister as well as how I knew he felt toward Mary and the kids. I've seen how he watches them whenever they're in the same room. Not like in a creeper way, but more of in a protective way. I always suspected he'd eventually claim Mary as his sister, but that it might take him time to get there. I don't know everything about his sister, but I know enough to know his dad violently killed her and then his mother made his life a living hell until Poseidon and Marie took him in.

I didn't know it at the time, but after each of Mary's kidnappings, Phoenix was down in our gym and would obliterate a gym bag or two as he took out his anger on it at Mary being hurt again. I'd known he was always protective of Nikki, Sadie, Susie, and Jordan, but that protectiveness pales in comparison to what I've seen him display this past month toward Mary and our kids.

Phoenix gives me a chin lift and I grin, happy that they both have each other now.

"Μαμά (Mom), are you okay?" Izzy asks as he puts down his jar of sprinkles on the counter. I have a feeling we'll be finding sprinkles all over for the next few months with how much the kids have been putting on the cookies today, but it's worth it.

Mary nods as she wipes her eyes again. "Yes, Sparks, I'm good." She hesitates and looks up at Phoenix, probably not sure how to explain their new relationship.

I clear my throat and the kids all turn back toward me. "Kids, do you guys remember how Uncle Smoke claimed Aunt Levi as his sister?"

They nod.

"And like how Uncle Axe and Uncle Punisher claimed Auntie MaeMae as their sister?" Ash asks, his eyes lighting up as he gets where I'm going with this. I still don't know why the kids only call Mae 'Auntie' and the others 'Aunt'. I know Jordan started it, since Mae is now technically his aunt, so maybe the other kids just followed suit.

I grin and nod. "Well, Uncle Phoenix just claimed your mom as his sister."

Shrieks of joy, which seem to be the norm for these three lately, ring out through the house as all three kids clamor down the bar stools and they all race toward Phoenix. Smiling at them, he crouches down and catches all of them in his arms. Cassie reaches up and places a kiss on his chin.

"Now you're really my uncle!" she giggles and I pretend not to notice Phoenix's eyes turn misty.

"That I am, Angel."

"Do you want to decorate cookies with us? We're making a bunch for the club, Santa, and after we're done with these, μαμά (mom) is going to show us how to make reindeer food for them when Santa comes tonight!" Izzy asks him excitedly and a soft look comes over Phoenix's face.

"Let me just take off my cut so it doesn't get dirty, then you can show me what to do. I'm not much of an artist, but I'll do my best."

Walking over to Mary, I wrap my arms around her, pulling her against my chest. "You good?" I whisper and feel her nod against me.

"So good," she whispers back and I can hear the tears in her voice. "I finally have a brother. Something I've wished for ever since I was a kid."

I tighten my arms around her and place a kiss on her shoulder. The sound of laughter has me looking up and my chest tightens as I see the kids already having fun decorating with Phoenix.

Mary pats my chest. "Let's join them before they decide to fully decorate him in flour," she says, as she tries to hide her laughter, but when Cassie wipes a dollop of frosting across Phoenix's nose, it escapes anyway. Her laughter gets louder when Phoenix rubs noses with Cassie, getting the frosting on her in the process.

"Okay, let's save the frosting for the cookies," Mary says through her laughter.

Pulling out my phone, I take a few more pictures of my family.

My chest tightens even more at that.

Finally. After nine years, I finally have the family I've always wanted with Mary. Sure, two of my kids aren't mine by blood, but I claim them as mine all the same.

A few hours later, I pull our SUV up to the clubhouse and shut off the engine. With how many boxes of cookies we have, it was just easier to do it this way. Not to mention the almost foot of snow we have on the ground would have made trekking up here difficult for Mary.

Getting out of the SUV, I open the back door and help the kids out. As soon as their feet hit the ground, they're racing toward the clubhouse.

"Slow down, be careful of ice," I call out as I round the SUV, watching to make sure none of them wipe out. Once they're inside, I open Mary's door, lift her in my arms and carefully carry her up the steps, mindful of her dress so I don't flash anyone. Ethan opens the door for me, and I pause before entering the clubhouse. "Help carry in all the containers in the back of the SUV, will ya?"

He gives me a chin lift and does as I ask.

Mary gasps as I cross the threshold and I stop, noting that the kids have stopped not too far in front of us as well. All four of them are staring at the transformed main room and I can't stop my grin as I watch their reactions. Mary wiggles in my arms and I lower her to the ground, but keep my arm around her waist since I still need to get her scooter out of the SUV.

I'd purposefully kept Mary and the kids away from the clubhouse since noon yesterday to be able to pull this off. At first, I'd balked when I was told I was expected to stay away too, but Levi and Mae made a very good point. This is our first Christmas together and that I shouldn't spend it away from them, even if it would have been to help create and decorate everything. I'd given Mae and Levi my requests, however I knew they'd make the Prospects do most of the things since they are both pregnant, but what's in front of me goes beyond my requests.

To my right, there's a giant tree that damn near reaches the ceiling with the star on it. Its limbs are decorated heavily with lights, garland, ornaments, and a ton of motorcycle themed ornaments as well. Garland drapes across the ceiling and there are also snowflakes hanging from the ceiling. Lights and Christmas decals are in every window, and it looks like they used that frost spray to add a more wintery feel. The pass through has been decorated and each table has a centerpiece consisting of a candle inside a small wreath. The tables all have what looks like three tablecloths on them – green on the bottom, then red, and then white ones overtop. It even looks like they put some sort of confetti on the tables, too. The fireplace mantle and the hearth are all decked out and there's stockings hung up on the mantle and the wall surrounding the fireplace. It looks like there's a stocking for everyone, not just the kids.

Cassie shrieks as she points at the walls and my eyebrows damn near disappear into my hairline.

Images of Santa's workshop and the North Pole are on each wall. I seriously hope they are those removeable decals decoration things and that someone didn't put all that effort into painting all of that only to have to paint over it after the holidays are over.

"This is why," Mary whispers and I wrap my arms around her, pulling her into me.

She doesn't have to continue, because I know what she's referring to. I had told her that I had a few surprises up my sleeves and that I wanted to spend the time this weekend getting to know my family better, which was true. I also told her that in order for one of my surprises to be done, we had to stay away from the clubhouse once we came back from lunch yesterday.

"This is why." I lean forward, kissing her forehead before leaning down to whisper in her ear. "There will be another one after supper, so I'll need you to play along."

Her brow furrows in confusion, but she nods. The door opens behind me and I usher the kids in further. Picking Mary back up, I walk her over to the table Levi,

Mae, and Elvira are sitting at and set her down on a chair. Giving her another kiss, I straighten, loving that she still has a stunned look on her face as she continues to look around the room.

"Gonna get your scooter for you. Be back in a bit, Siren." She absently nods and all the ladies smile widely as I give them nods of thanks. I'll need to thank them officially later.

Chapter 4

Cassie

"Holy cow... We're in a winter wonderland."

Both Ash and Izzy nod and I squeal in happiness before running over to the nearest wall to look at the Christmas scenes better. I reach out to touch the pretty walls, but Ash catches my hand, and I look down at my feet.

That's right. We can't touch pretties. I always forget, but Ash never makes me feel bad for forgetting.

"It's alright, she can touch the walls, Ash," a voice comes from behind us.

Turning around, I look up to see Uncle Timber walking up to us and he crouches down, which makes me happy because it hurts my neck to look up at all of them for too long. They are all so tall.

"But it looks so expensive," Ash tells him, and the worry in his voice has me looking back down at my shoes out of habit. Uh oh. Because of me, we're going to get in trouble.

Fear makes my hands shake. I'm used to that tone in Ash's voice. I've always listened to Ash because he always watches out for me and protects me. When I asked him about it, Ash told me I was his princess, and he was my knight. That he'd always protect me. Him and Izzy both.

I don't want to do anything that would get him in trouble, but I think I just did. Even if Uncle Timber did say it was alright. He was prol...prob...prolly just saying that. I don't want Daddy and μαμά (mom) to get mad at us. I frown. I wish I could say the Greek word for Daddy, but it's too hard for me to say. I hope I can say it right soon. Patch is the bestest Daddy ever and I don't want to make him mad at me.

"Oh, Angel."

I look up at Uncle Timber and blink to try and make my tears go away.

He makes a weird sound and then scoops me up in his arms. I bury my head in his chest, wanting to hide even though I want to look at all the pretty decorations. I've never seen so many pretty things like this for Christmas before. Well, I saw them on TV but that's different. After a bit, Uncle Timber's rough hands raise my chin to look up at him as he leans back.

"Angel, you are not in trouble, and neither are your brothers. The decals are not expensive, and you can touch them if you want. You can even rearrange them if you want, too."

I stare at him. I can... change them?

He smiles and nods.

Ooops. I think I did a μαμά (mom). Daddy said that when μαμά (mom) has to take her pain pills, she sometimes says things out loud without real...realzing it.

"You can change them, move them around, whatever. We put these up for you guys to have fun with. However, the other decorations are just that. Decorations. If you want to look at something closer, let one of us adults know and we can show you, but you should not touch those ones. Okay?"

I nod, getting excited again. "Promise, Uncle Timber."

He kisses my forehead, and I giggle as I feel his whiskers tickle my skin. He sets me down and when I step closer to the wall, I can't stop my hand from shaking. Looking over my shoulder at him again, he nods and I smile, quickly turning back toward the wall.

Izzy giggles as he comes and joins me. A moment later, Lindsey and Sadie join us as well.

We move around the polar bears and the elves, laughing as we make them dance in the air as we play. Izzy makes up stories as we play, too. He's great at telling stories. Ash sometimes draws pictures to go along with Izzy's stories. I love when they do that.

Someone taps my shoulders, and I turn around, smiling when I see Daddy crouched behind us.

"Daddy! Look at the scene we made." I point to the one we just finished. There's a campfire that's out in the woods and a bunch of animals are sitting around it. We put a snowman in it too, but we can't put him too close to the fire or he'd melt. It reminded me of the movie, *Frosty the Snowman*, that we watched last night on TV.

"That's pretty cool. Is that Frosty?" he asks as he points to the snowman and I nod.

"Yup. And that's the rabbit that was in his hat."

"You guys did an awesome job decorating, but now it's time to eat. You can decorate more after supper."

My tummy grumbles and Daddy smiles. He picks me up and I snuggle into him. I still can't believe Daddy lets me snuggle him, but I'm glad he does. He gives the bestest snuggles, even though Uncle Bear insists his are better. His snuggles are good too, but they aren't Daddy's snuggles.

Daddy carries me over to the counter where Auntie MaeMae, Aunt Levi, Granny Elvira, and μαμά (mom) always set out food and my eyes widen at everything in front of us. There's so much food that the counter is full and they had to add two more tables to hold it all.

I eye the big turkey that's in the middle of one of the tables. I've always loved turkey, but Stephan never let us have much. When he did, it was only the part that μαμά calls the breast meat, but I don't like the breast meat. It was usually pretty dry unless μαμά put gravy on it. I only know the other parts, the juicy ones, taste good because μαμά would sneak us pieces of them when Stephan was away at work. But μαμά said we couldn't have too much otherwise Stephan would notice and get mad.

"Do we have to eat the dry part? Or can we get the juicy parts of the turkey?"

No one answers me but a lot of them look angry. I turn my head into Daddy's chest.

Did I do something wrong again?

Chapter 5
Ash

SILENCE MEETS CASSIE'S WORDS. My chest hurts when her face falls and she turns into Dad's chest as she tries to hide. Izzy makes a small whimper, and he steps closer to me. I wrap my arm around him like I'd seen Dad do when one of us gets upset.

I know where Cassie's mind went. Both of their minds, actually.

At home, it's easier for them to remember they aren't going to get in trouble for asking for something, but here at the clubhouse? They both still get lots of what Dad says are 'triggers'.

Dad's face turns angry before he exhales heavily a couple of times and then his face calms slightly, but I can still tell his jaw is tense.

I know now that when he looks like that it's because he's furious at Stephan and what he put us through. The others in the club get similar looks on their faces sometimes too. They all hate what Stephan did to us, especially to μαμά (mom). In fact, several of them look really mad right now and I bet they heard what Cassie said.

However, I know none of them would ever hurt us, even if they do get mad at us for something. But Cassie and Izzy still fall back into old habits as μαμά (mom) says when they think they'll get in trouble. Glancing over at μαμά (mom), I can tell by the look in her eyes that she's remembering how Stephan took almost all the dark meat at Thanksgiving. Not even having our great-grandparents there stopped him from doing it. He pulled stuff like that all the time.

I know it's just food, but Stephan limited what we could and could not have. He never starved us, but after hearing the other grownups talking, he made sure we didn't get everything we needed. Once I heard Aunt Levi say Stephan probably kept us weak on purpose as another control method. It took a while for me to realize what she meant, because at first I didn't understand. However, after talking with Dad, it finally clicked and looking back, that's exactly what he did.

Still, in the time we've been living here with Dad, both Cassie and Izzy have opened up and are more vocal of their needs and wants. So much so that I'm actually proud of Cassie for asking for what she wants instead of just taking what she was given.

"It's okay," I whisper to Izzy and Dad looks up slightly, his eyes locking with mine and he nods.

"You're right, Ash, it is okay." He pauses as he lifts Cassie's chin to make her look at him. "Άγγελε (Angel), it's okay to ask for things you want. If you want the juicy parts of the turkey, then that's what you're going to get. You want mashed potatoes drenched in gravy? You're gonna get it. We will never limit any foods unless you end up developing an allergy to something. You will never get in trouble for asking for something, okay?"

Cassie smiles, though it isn't her full smile that we've been seeing more and more of, and nods. "Yes, Daddy."

Dad kisses her on the forehead and then turns toward Uncle Thor, who I can tell is upset at what Cassie was implying. Uncle Thor who steps up behind the table with the turkey carver, or whatever it's called, and clears his throat as he looks around the room.

"This is the first Christmas our club has been as big as it has ever been. Some of us starting families or having gained family members. We've had Old Ladies and children join us and some of our brothers have expanded their families by claiming sisters."

I look around and smile when Uncle Phoenix wraps an arm around μαμά (mom). In response, she hugs his waist as she leans against his shoulder. Looking around some more, my smile widens even further when I see Uncle Axe and Aunt Susie hugging Mae and I giggle along with my brother when Uncle Smoke pulls Aunt Nikki, Aunt Levi, Aunt Sasha, Uncle Alexei and Uncle Ethan all in for a big, yet squished, hug. Several of us laugh even harder when Uncle Bear comes up behind Uncle Smoke and hugs all of them as well.

Uncle Thor's smile widens as he looks around the room. "Next year we'll grow even more as we'll be welcoming five new lives into our club." He pauses and looks over to Aunt Levi who is smiling and rubbing her belly. Uncle Dragon gently pulls her out of Smoke's embrace and wraps an arm around her, kissing her forehead. "It's my hope that our club will continue to grow strong and expand. While you all know that I'm not religious, there is always one prayer that I use whenever I ride, and since I know some of us will be traveling to see their families for the holiday, I hope you'll join me in saying it."

Confused, I look around the room and am surprised when every member of the club seems to stand taller with their heads slightly bent and most are holding their hands together in front of them. I turn back toward Uncle Thor who is also standing taller, his head slightly bent, and one hand clasping the wrist of his other in front of him. Then as one, they all start speaking in unison.

"May the sun rise in front of me, the rain fall behind me and the wind follow me.

May the angels guard my travels for they know what is ahead of me.

Keep me safe through rolling hills and swirling turns.

Let the eagle guide me to the mountain tops.

Let the moon's light guide me through the night.

Lord, thank you for letting me be a biker."

Uncle Thor looks around when they all raise their heads and he smirks. "Now, let's eat."

After finishing my food and putting my dishes in the kitchen, I sit down and look around the main room. Cassie, Izzy, Lindsey, Sadie and even Jordan have started to rearrange the Christmas scenes again on the walls that I now know Auntie MaeMae was behind. I overheard her saying that she wanted to do something that would entertain the kids and to maybe save the more expensive decorations from their playful hands.

Everyone's mingling and something in my chest warms as I watch them hug each other and wish each other a Merry Christmas as well as wishing each other safe travels. Though most of the guys do that thing where they shake hands and clasp each other's shoulders. Watching them, I think I may be starting to understand a bit of what Dad has talked about regarding the club. That not only is everyone in the club his friend, but they are also his family. His chosen or found family as Aunt Levi calls it.

I turn, watching Dad and μαμά talk with Auntie MaeMae and Uncle Timber, and nod to myself.

This is where we're meant to be.

And when I grow older, I want to be a part of the club, just like Dad.

Chapter 6

Izzy

I'M REARRANGING ANOTHER CHRISTMAS scene with Cassie on the walls when I hear bells jingling.

"Did you hear that?" Cassie asks me, her voice a whisper as she looks around, her eyes wide.

"Yeah, I did," I reply, trying to keep my voice just as quiet in case it happens again.

And then it does.

The jingling sound gets louder as the room quiets down.

"I wonder what that could be," Uncle Dragon says from the couch near us.

Cassie and I turn back toward each other, and I'm sure my eyes are as wide as hers.

"Could it be Santa?" she asks and I shrug. I thought Santa only came after we went to bed.

Loud stomps come from the hallway and both of us turn. My jaw drops in surprise.

Santa.

Santa Claus is really here.

Here. In the clubhouse.

"Ho ho ho ho!" he bellows and I laugh along with Cassie and a few of the others as his belly shakes. Over his shoulder, he's holding a big red bag. And I mean a *big* red bag. "I heard there are a few children here that have been very good this year. So good, that I decided to stop by before I headed out tonight."

He sets the red bag down and then sits in one of the leather armchairs as all of us kids gather around in front of him. Like me, a lot of them are shocked, but we're all still excited.

Cassie's beside me, but I don't see Ash. Going up on my tip toes, I frown when I notice Ash still sitting back where he was. After a few moments, Dad finally encourages him to come up and join us. Happy that he's joining us.

Santa laughs at something, and for a moment, it sounds familiar, but I shake it off as I turn back toward him.

"Now, let's see who this first present is for," he says, his voice deep, but also cheerful. He smiles as he reads the tag and then he strokes his long white beard as he looks at all of us. "This is for a Miss Cassie," he says as he hands Cassie the present.

Wait, how did he know which one of the girls was Cassie? Then I remember that Santa has magic. Knowing which kid is which and if they've been naughty or nice is part of that.

Cassie flings herself at Santa, hugging him and thanking him before taking the present.

"Μαμά (Mom)! Santa gave me a present!" she cries as she runs over to her. Μαμά (Mom) leans forward, smiling widely as Cassie shows her the pretty glitter wrapping paper and the bright pink bow and ribbons.

While we've gotten a few presents over the years, I know μαμά (mom) had to get some of the cheapest wrapping paper and bows because of how much Stephan had limited her money. The only reason I know about that is because one time when we went shopping for Cassie's birthday, I had heard μαμά (mom) complaining when she thought I couldn't hear her. She wished she could afford the really pretty paper, ribbons, and bows and that she hated her spending limit. That she wished she could give us more. Instead of the pretty paper, ribbons, and bows, she bought a big roll of that brown craft paper stuff and drew on it herself before adding a simple bow to it. I never cared that she had a limit, I loved all the presents she, Cassie, and Ash would get me because they came from them. The only time we got pretty wrapping paper and bows was when Santa brought us gifts.

I turn back to Santa when I hear him call my name and my eyes widen when he hands me a large box, but he doesn't let go. Even with him holding it, the box is heavy. What could it be?

"I think you'll need help carrying this one, Little Man. Which one of these men is your dad?"

I glance back over my shoulder, barely holding in my excitement and smile when I see Dad's already heading toward us.

"I am."

Grinning, my chest warms when he says he's my dad. I love that he treats Cassie and me the same as he treats Ash. He really doesn't care that we aren't related by blood, but he claims us as his.

I let Dad take the present and then fling myself at Santa, hugging him tight. "Thank you, Santa!"

He chuckles and then I'm wrapped in a giant bear hug. "You're welcome, Little Man."

Stepping back, I almost run over to Dad who's moved to sit at a table along with μαμά (mom) and Cassie. Dad lifts me onto his lap when I get to him and my fingers itch to tear away at the wrapping paper to see what Santa got me, but I force myself to wait since the others are too.

Looking back at Santa, I realize Ash is the last one to receive a present, and I can't help but freeze. For some reason, Stephan was always meaner to Ash on his birthday and at Christmas than he was to Cassie and me. A lot of times, whatever he got would be broken or destroyed—either before he really got to play with whatever it was or he did it when everyone was sleeping. When we woke up, Stephan was always there and whenever Ash would cry, Stephan got a weird smile on his face. I never liked it.

Dad's hand rubs up and down my back. "What's wrong?"

A weird sound comes from μαμά (mom) and I look over my shoulder at her.

"Stephan was always worse toward Ash because he wasn't his," she whispers. "After it first happened, we tried to not leave his things lying around during the day and at night, we tried to hide them as best as we could. If Stephan managed to get his hands on them or find them, he ruined them and always made sure he was there when it was discovered what he'd done."

Dad's body stiffens under mine and I lean further into Dad's chest when I realize some people around us heard what she'd said, too. I look over at Ash and realize Santa's staring at us. Uh-oh. Did Santa hear us too? Did Ash?

"Asher," Santa says and for a moment, his voice sounds a lot like the club members when they're upset. Their voices always seem harder, with an edge to it and I'm surprised to hear it from Santa.

"Asher," he repeats. "I know you haven't always been given the chance to enjoy some of my presents for very long, but I know that isn't the case anymore. I hope you like these, but like some of the others, your box is a little heavy."

Santa pulls a big box out of his bag. Uncle Phoenix steps forward, takes the box from Santa and then he guides Ash over to our table. Ash has a stunned, but shocked look on his face as Phoenix lifts him so that he's sitting on his lap and able to reach the box easier.

Someone claps their hands and I realize it was Santa, who is now standing and smiling at all of us.

"All of you were so good, waiting for everyone to get their present. Go ahead and open them up!"

Excitedly, I rip into the wrapping paper in front of me but then stop when I realize what Santa got me.

"Oh my gosh." I can barely believe it.

A week or so ago, I was talking to Uncle Judge about wanting to build my own bike when I got older. Maybe even restore an old car. How did Santa find out? I didn't tell him in my letter that I wanted a model engine kit so I could start learning, but somehow, he knew.

"Holy cow. Izzy, that is so cool," Dad says as he looks closer at the box.

"What did you get, Izzy?" μαμά asks me and I turn the box so she can see as I rip off the rest of the paper.

"A model engine kit," I tell her excitedly. "And it looks like it will run when I'm finished with it!"

Μαμά (Mom) stares at the box, her mouth opening and closing, but nothing comes out for a bit.

"Oh my," she says quietly with her hand over her mouth as she stares at the box in front of me. After a few moments, she reaches up and dries her eyes and cheeks. My chest tightens at seeing her tears. She must notice me worrying because she smiles. "It's okay, Sparks. They're happy tears." I relax at that. I hate seeing my μαμά cry.

"**Μαμά** (Mom), Santa got me butterflies and fairies!" Cassie says excitedly when she gets all her wrapping paper off her box and I smile when I see what it is.

Santa gave her a kit where she can make her own fairy and butterfly garden.

Turning toward Ash, I frown when I realize he's just staring at his box and hasn't opened it yet.

"What's wrong, Ash?" Uncle Phoenix asks him as he places a hand on his shoulder and pulls him into his chest a bit more.

My chest hurts at the pain on Ash's face and I turn. I think I know what his problem is, but maybe Santa can help him. If the words come from him instead of Dad or μαμά again, then maybe he'll believe it.

Chapter 7
Patch

Izzy shifts on my lap but my focus is on Ash. He's staring at his present with longing and pain. Phoenix's gaze catches mine and I nod. Putting my hand on Ash's shoulder, I squeeze it gently.

"It's okay, Ash. No one is going to take whatever Santa gave you away. Nor are they going to break it. This is for you and you deserve to be happy.

He looks up at me and my chest tightens at the sadness in his eyes. "But I don't... I mean..." He pauses as he looks behind me and then back to me. "I know..."

It takes a moment, and then it clicks. He knows there is no Santa. I'm going to have to ask Mary what happened. I have a sneaky suspicion that Stephan told Ash there was no Santa and my guess is that Ash was probably younger than Cassie is now when he found out. Based on what Mary just said about what Stephan would do to Ash, I'm going to bet he's scared that whatever is in the box might get taken away from him, but that's something he never has to worry about. Not anymore.

"It's okay," I repeat, but movement behind me has me turning to see Santa pulling up a chair next to us.

Santa and Ash look at each other for a while, neither of them saying anything. It's like they're having a silent conversation that the rest of us aren't privy to. After a few moments, Santa gives Ash a soft smile and nods his head. Ash's smile is slower, but finally, a real smile lights up his face and he tears at the wrapping paper which reveals a plain white box.

He opens the lid and his jaw drops, shock written all over his face. Phoenix lifts him up so that he's kneeling carefully on his lap and able to see into the box better. Almost reverently, Ash starts pulling items out of the box. There are books on animal anatomy which Carter, our town's vet, probably helped pick out. Then he pulls out multiple sketchbooks and coloring books that are more like the adult ones, but these ones are about various animals. Next, he pulls out a few packs of what look to be the really good kind of colored pencils, markers, and charcoal pencils.

Ash climbs down off Phoenix's lap and launches himself at Santa. His arms wrap around Ash in a bear hug. I hear them talking quietly, but even this close to them, I can't make out what they're saying. Santa laughs and when Ash pulls back, he's smiling widely.

Santa sets Ash back down on Phoenix's lap as he stands and then he goes to each one of the kids, talking to them quietly and the kids each give him a hug before thanking him again. He picks up his now empty red bag, and winks at the kids.

"Be good now and make sure to go to bed on time. I'll be back later tonight once you're all asleep with the rest of your presents."

Cassie makes a sound and when I turn toward her, I chuckle when I see her eyes wide and her mouth is dropped in surprise. "More presents?" Her little brow wrinkles in confusion. "We get more than one?"

My smile faulters as anger instantly runs through my veins and I fight not to show it or to have my muscles tighten. Since Izzy's still sitting on my lap, I don't want him to feel how pissed I am. Mary hugs Cassie tightly to her, her eyes closed as she whispers quietly with her. If I weren't staring at her, I would have missed the couple of tears that run down Mary's cheeks. My gaze catches with Santa's as he pauses on his way to the hallway leading out back. He tilts his head at me and I return it. Then, he disappears down the hallway.

Clearing my throat, they all turn toward me and I wink, hoping they can't see any of the anger I'm trying to hide.

"Yup, Santa's got more presents for you but those will come later, like he said and you'll be able to open them tomorrow morning. You'll also get some more presents from μαμά (mom) and me, too." I pause, dramatically tapping my chin. "I'm even thinking that we should continue my family's tradition, too."

"What's that?" Izzy asks as he twists in my lap to look up at me. Mary smiles and nods, probably guessing which one I'm talking about since she spent so many Christmases with us growing up. Her dad even took to doing it as well.

"I think that when we get to the house, you all can choose one present to open. However, the rest will need to wait for tomorrow morning."

Izzy wraps his arms around me, hugging me tight as he buries his head in the crook of my neck. "This is the best Christmas ever."

I tighten my arms around him.

I couldn't agree more.

A few hours later, I round the kids up and carry Mary out to our SUV. Within minutes, we're back home and I can't stop smiling at how excited the kids are as they talk about how they can't wait to play with their presents.

Hanging up our coats, I know the kids have spotted one of my surprises when their chatter instantly dies down.

"How did you get Bear to dress up as Santa?" Mary whisper to me, unaware of the impending surprise.

I chuckle and shake my head. "He actually offered to do it. He loves kids so I wouldn't be surprised if he becomes our resident Santa going forward."

I frown then, wondering if Bear was actually able to get a hold of his daughter this time. He and his wife divorced years ago. From the rumor I heard, his ex played dirty during the divorce and presented false evidence. She got away with it because the judge that oversaw their case hated the club. His ex got full custody of their daughter and he only got supervised visitation. However, over the years, his ex poisoned his daughter's mind, telling her lies about him and the club. He hasn't seen or talked to his daughter since her sixteenth birthday. That was ten years ago, I think. He calls her every holiday and on her birthday but each time, he just gets her voicemail and she never returns the calls to my knowledge.

Shaking my head, I slip off my shoes and follow Mary into the living room. She stops in front of me and looks over her shoulder at me, her eyes wide with shock.

"Did you do this?" she mouths and I step forward, wrapping my arms around her.

Her body is a bit tense and I hope I haven't overstepped. Especially because I still have one more surprise coming, but that will be in the morning.

I lean in, inhaling her cherry blossom scent. "I had a little help setting this up while we were at the clubhouse. It won't be like this every year, but this year I wanted to do something special for all of you as our first Christmas together."

Mary's body relaxes as she melts into me and my worries ease.

Turning, I smile down at the kids as they take in all the presents surrounding the Christmas tree. Earlier, there'd been a small pile for each kid under the tree, but Sasha had set out more for me while we were at the clubhouse.

"Okay, kiddos. You can each pick one present to open tonight."

Excited giggles erupt out of Cassie and Izzy as they damn near dive into the pile of presents as they try to decide which one to pick. Ash is more quiet, but just as excited. It seems that whatever he talked Bear about seemed to help him. Giving Mary a little squeeze, I tilt my head toward the tree.

"What about you, Siren? Want to pick out a present too?"

Mary hesitates, and I almost think she's going to say no.

"Come on, μαμά (mom)! Pick one! Pick one!" Izzy says excitedly, and soon, Cassie and even Ash get in on it.

Mary laughs softly and finally nods. "Okay kiddos, but how about you guys pick one out for me to open."

The kids immediately start looking for which ones are Mary's.

I take the time to help Mary settle down onto the couch and I move her scooter off to the side so it's out of the way. Pulling out my phone, I snap a few pictures of the kids. Soon I'm going to have to download all the photos with how many I've taken the past few days. I'll need to figure out which ones to print out too so we can frame them.

After a few moments, the kids hand Mary a present and I'm surprised, though I shouldn't be, when they hand one to me too.

Mary winks at me. "You aren't the only one that has surprises up their sleeve."

Grinning, I turn back toward the kids. "Have you guys picked one out to open?"

"Yup!" Cassie exclaims and both Izzy and Ash nod their heads.

"Okay, go ahead and open them up."

They all tear into the wrapping paper, much more comfortable now than they had been earlier.

"No way," Ash says quietly as he reveals a new racing game that he's been wanting.

Izzy got a working engine brick set and Cassie got a princess brick set.

"Thank you, μαμά (mom) and Dad!" Ash says and the others chime in, saying their thanks as well.

"What did you guys get?" Izzy asks Mary and me.

Neither one of us has opened our presents yet, so we both start opening them. Mine is from all three of the kids and if I'm not mistaken, the present Mary's opening is one that's from me and the kids.

Opening the box, I'm surprised to find a custom leather wallet that's on a chain that I can hook onto my belt for when I'm riding. Running my fingers over the burned in images, I smile at the butterfly, motorcycle, and the cardecus that decorate the wallet.

"Thank you, kids, I love it."

"Oh my gosh," Mary says quietly, and I turn toward her. Her hand is covering her mouth and I realize the present she opened *is* the one I thought it was. It's a mother's ring with all five of our birthstones on it. The kids helped me pick out the design.

"Did we get the right size?" Ash asks her.

She takes out the ring and slides it onto her ring finger on her right hand. I breathe a sigh of relief when she nods and beams at us. I'd measured her finger when she'd been sleeping one night.

"Perfect fit. Thank you, I love it."

Chapter 8
Patch

ABOUT AN HOUR LATER, it's time for bed and the kids groan when we announce its bedtime.

"Well, if you don't go to sleep, then Santa won't come," Mary says and Cassie perks up.

"Wait! We need to put out the reindeer food and Santa's cookies and milk first."

Getting up off the couch, I bring Mary's scooter over to her and we all head into the kitchen. Reaching into the cupboard, I rummage through our stack of holiday plates.

"Which plate do you guys want to use for Santa?"

"There should be one of Santa's face in there. We picked it out at the store the other day," Mary tells me and I pull it out after finding it, setting it on the island. Mary opens the plastic container that holds the cookies the kids had previously set aside for Santa and she hands it to the kids. They load up the plate while I grab a glass out of the cupboard and fill it with milk.

"Where should we put them?" Ash asks as he looks back at the living room.

"How about we put them on the coffee table?" I suggest, and I pick up the plate, carrying both back into the living room.

Setting the plate down on the center of the table and then grab a coaster for the milk.

"Get your boots and coats back on, kids, and then we'll sprinkle the reindeer food outside," I tell them as Mary hands me three baggies filled with raw uncooked oats and some red and green colored sugar.

Mary stays near the door, phone out and ready for pictures while I head out into the front yard with the kids. I help them spread out the reindeer food, stopping Cassie just in time so that she doesn't dump the whole bag at once.

Scooping Cassie up in my arms, I tickle her and boop noses with her as we head back inside. "Now to get you all tucked in so Santa can come."

She reaches up, booping my nose with her finger. "You and μαμά (mom) have to go to sleep too."

I chuckle. "Yup, we'll go to sleep to." Though I have plans for my Siren before we go to sleep, but Cassie doesn't need to know that.

"Can you read *The Night Before Christmas* again?" Izzy asks as we take off our coats and boots again.

"Yes, but you all have to get into your pajamas and brush your teeth first."

The kids race to the stairs and thankfully, they slow down enough that we don't have to yell at them for running on the stairs.

"Hold up," Mary calls out when they reach the landing and they turn back toward her. She holds out three gift bags. "I got us all Christmas themed pajamas. They're already washed, so you can wear them tonight."

They eagerly descend the stairs again and rip out the tissue paper, pulling out their pajamas. Ash's has cats and dogs with Santa hats on them. Cassie's has Olaf from the movie *Frozen* on them. Izzy's... I'm almost positive Izzy's pajamas were custom made. There are snowmen wearing leather jackets and motorcycles on his pajamas.

"Awesome! Thank you!" Izzy shouts before almost running to Mary, giving her a hug and then he does the same to me.

"Okay, now get your tushies upstairs and ready for bed," Mary tells them and they excitedly head upstairs.

Walking over to her, I kiss her and then lift her in my arms, carrying her upstairs. "And what are our pajamas?" I ask her, my voice husky as thoughts of what I'm going to do to her later run through my head.

She gives me a sly, saucy grin. "You'll just have to wait and find out."

Fuck. Now I'm imagining her in some sexy lingerie. She laughs at me as I take deep breaths, apparently knowing my struggle. Fuck... This hard on better go down before story time.

After reading three Christmas stories, we finally got the kids to settle down for bed. However, I bet we'll be woken up bright and early with how excited they are to see what Santa brings them.

Reaching the bottom of the stairs, I set Mary down next to her scooter.

"Do you think we're safe to set things out?" she asks me, her voice just barely a whisper so that the kids don't hear her.

Glancing up at their closed doors, I nod, hesitantly. "I think we're probably okay. I know they're excited, but I don't think they'll come out of their rooms until morning."

I head to the closet we've commandeered to hold the extra presents from us, as well as what will be from Santa, and unlock the door.

"How about I bring them over and you can arrange them around the tree?" I ask her and she nods, pivoting her scooter before heading over to the tree.

It takes a bit with how many presents we have, but finally, they're all spread out around the tree.

Well, almost all of them.

Nervously, I scratch the back of my neck and she narrows her eyes at me before shaking her head and sighing.

"Let me guess, you have more surprises?" she asks, cocking an eyebrow at me as she smirks.

"I may have gone... a little overboard with wanting this Christmas to be special." Fuck, my face feels like it's probably as red as a tomato.

She wraps her arms around my waist and I lean down, kissing her. She pulls back after a few moments, a soft smile on her face.

"You're under the mistletoe, Santa." Mary winks and I lean down to kiss her again. I'd purposefully put it here with this exact intention. Unfortunately, the kiss ends far to soon as she pulls back, breaking the kiss. I rest my forehead against hers.

"As long as every year isn't this extravagant, then it's okay."

Exhaling, tension starts to leech out of my shoulders. I'd been worried she'd be mad at me for this. I shake my head. "It won't be like this every year."

She reaches up, wrapping her arms around my neck, and I bite back a groan at feeling her curves pressed against me. Leaning down, I kiss her harder this time and she moans into my mouth. My hands grip her hips tighter, and I pull her harder against me, but it isn't enough.

Mary pulls away slightly, panting as she tries to catch her breath. "What about the kids?" she whispers.

Nipping her lip, I listen, but don't hear anything but our breathing. "I think they're asleep by now. Besides, none of our kids are quiet when they walk. Not anymore. We'll hear them if they come out of their rooms."

Mary chuckles, which turns into a moan as I kiss down her neck. Her fingers thread through my hair and I damn near loose it when she rolls her hips against me. Picking her up and turnings us so that her back is against the wall, I help her keep steady since she no longer has her scooter under her leg. Pressing a leg in between hers, she moans, rocking her pelvis against my thigh. I run my fingers through her hair before fisting it and gently leaning her head to the side. Her moans deepen when I kiss down her neck and my other hand teases her nipple through her dress and bra.

My sexy Siren whimpers and grinds her hips against me. My hand trails down her chest and stomach before reaching the edge of her dress. Slowly, I slide the material up her leg but I leave my hand on her thigh, teasing her with my touch.

"Luke, please," she begs before biting on her lip.

"Is my Siren wet for me? Is your pussy greedy for my touch?"

She whimpers again. "Yes, please touch me, Luke."

Once again, I slowly trail my fingers up her inner thigh until I reach her hot center. I rub over her clit through the silky material of her panties and groan when I find them already drenched. Slipping a finger inside her panties, I groan even louder.

"Fuck, you're so wet, Siren."

Kissing her deeply, I tease her clit and she moans into my mouth. I rub my fingers in a circle over her clit, pressing a bit harder and faster. Her hands claw at my shoulders before she reaches down and her fingers dip under the hem of my shirt. I press myself harder against her when her nails lightly scratch my back. Fuck, I love when her claws come out. I love wearing her marks.

My cock is as hard as steel, but I can't come yet.

Breaking the kiss, I pepper her jaw and neck with kisses until I get to the crook of her neck. I lick her sensitive spot, loving when a shiver runs through her. Judging by her increased whimpers and how jerky her movements have become, she's close.

I press a little harder against her clit while my other hand threads through her hair, pulling her head to the side again. "Come for me, Siren," I command before biting down on her neck, just hard enough to drive her crazy and help push her over the edge, but not enough to break skin.

She slaps a hand over her mouth as she shatters in my arms and I back off of the pressure on her clit, softly stroking it to prolong her orgasm.

After a few moments, her body sags against me slightly. She raises her hand, cupping my jaw before going up on her toes and kissing me.

Breaking the kiss, I press my forehead to hers as I fight not to just take her here and now.

"You better set out the rest of your surprises because I have plans for you tonight," she says, her voice deeper and huskier in the wake of her orgasm. I moan when she reaches down and rubs her hand over my cock through the jeans.

"Fuck, Siren." My hips jerk, not able to resist.

Reluctantly, I step back slightly, but not before stealing one more kiss, and I move her scooter so that it's within reach again.

"I want you on your hands and knees when I get back in our room."

Her eyes flare and her pupils dilate at my words and she smiles saucily at me. "Don't keep me waiting too long."

Using her scooter, she slips out of my arms, and heads to our bedroom. I bite back a groan as my eyes zero in on how that dress hugs her perfect ass. Halfway there, she looks over her shoulder and winks at me, catching me staring at her.

When she disappears out of sight, I shake myself internally and head to the garage.

Previously, I had stored the extra gifts at Bear's and when I'd found out he was going to play Santa, I'd asked if a Prospect could get them from his house and bring them over while he was doing his thing. Currently, they're under a tarp along the back wall of the garage, hidden from view by my truck since the SUV is parked on the far left side of the garage and my truck is on the right.

Pulling off the tarp and folding it back up, I get to work carrying in the extra presents. There's a few where they'll have to come out here to get in the morning, but the rest I arrange as neatly as I can around the tree.

Twenty minutes later, I step back and am happy with how everything is laid out. I eat a couple of the cookies and the rest, I hide in a cupboard high up where the kids can't get them before polishing off the milk.

Now, to find my Siren.

Chapter 9
Mary

As soon as I round the corner leading to the hallway and out of sight of Luke, I hurry a little faster to our bedroom and shut the door. It will take a bit of time to do what I want to do, and I don't want Luke to see me before I'm ready.

Heading to my dresser, I pull out the outfit that I'd previously set aside and head into the bathroom. It takes a bit of maneuvering, but I finally get my zipper undone on my dress and strip it off. My bra and underwear quickly follow. After doing my business, I freshen up a bit.

An excited thrill races up my spine as I start to put on my outfit. This isn't the first time I've worn lingerie for Luke, but it is the first time that I'll be dressed up like this.

I slip on the green thong and then slip on the little green dress with red trim and red accents. Well, I guess *dress* is a bit of an overstatement. It's barely long enough to cover my ass and the top is so revealing that my nipples are barely contained in the 'bra' section of the dress.

Turning in the mirror, I make sure everything looks good with my outfit. I spritz a little perfume on and even though I don't need to, I touch up my makeup a little. I know Luke says I don't need to wear it. That I look pretty by just being me. However, I want tonight to be special, so I get to work with my makeup and then run a comb through my hair.

Glancing at my phone, I panic when I realize it's been almost fifteen minutes already, but when I head back in our room, I breathe out a sigh of relief that Luke isn't in here yet.

Scooting over to our bed, I pull off the comforter and sheet, folding them up and setting them on the armchair. I check our 'toy' drawer to make sure everything is still there and stocked in case we decide to use anything, but it's still the same as when I checked yesterday. I'd made sure everything was cleaned and charged, including the new additions I'd gotten when I went into town with the ladies the day after we handled my demons.

Scooting over to the bed, I climb onto my hands and knees, making sure that my cast is semi propped up and wait. However, instead of facing the head of the bed, I'm facing toward the door. Luke didn't cum earlier when he teased me and I want to make sure he cums at least twice tonight.

My nerves start to skyrocket as I wait, and I hope it isn't too long before Luke comes back.

A few minutes later, the door opens and Luke groans before quickly shutting the door and locking it. Internally I do a little happy dance at the desire in his eyes.

"Seems Santa left me a special kind of present."

A shiver races through me at his deeper, huskier tone. He crosses the room and leans down. One hand cups my face before he kisses me deeply, while the other hand traces down my neck to my breasts and then he teases it along my cleavage. Reaching forward, I rub his cock through his jeans.

"Mmmm, I must have been really good this year," he moans as my fingers work to unbuckle his jeans. Getting his zipper down, I reach inside and moan when I realize he went commando. Pulling out his cock, I lean forward licking the precum off the tip, pulling another moan out of him at the action. Taking him into my mouth, Luke curses.

"Fuck, Mary. Your mouth feels so good."

Luke reaches down, massaging one of my breasts and tweaking my nipple as I suck him deep into my throat and swallow. He curses again and another hand tangles in my hair. He holds my head steady and starts pumping his hips, fucking my mouth. I moan, loving when he does this. From my past, I never thought I'd love giving blow jobs again, not to mention letting him control me while doing so, but with Luke it's different.

Hollowing my cheeks, I suck on him harder. My pussy grows wetter from getting him off and from him teasing my breasts. His rhythm stutters, signaling he's close. He tweaks my nipple which has me moaning and he curses again before plunging back down my throat and ropes of cum shoot down my throat.

I swallow every drop, not wanting to spill any. When he's done, I lick his cock, making sure I got everything.

"Fuck, Mary."

He pulls me up so I'm on my knees and slams his lips down on mine as he holds me close.

"Fuck, lay down, Mary. Let me see my Christmas present."

Carefully, I lay down and he adjusts the pillow so my leg is propped up again.

He moans when I lay down, and he starts fisting his cock. "Fucking perfect. You are absolutely fucking gorgeous, Mary."

He crawls over me, running his hands up and down my body as he does. He places kisses at the edge of my dress on my breasts and kisses up my chest and neck. Running my hands up his back, I damn near growl in irritation as I fist his shirt. I want to feel his skin.

"You have too much clothing on," I whine and he flashes me his sexy smirk.

"Can't have that now, can we? Especially with you looking as sexy as you are."

He pulls back and quickly strips before crawling over me again. This time, I pull him tight against me when he kisses me. Leaning on one arm, his other caresses my breasts again, squeezing and tweaking my nipples just how I like it. Moaning, I push up harder into him. I feel like I'm going to combust. I need him so much. I had planned to take this much slower, but damn, I need him in me n ow.

"Please, Luke. I need you in me."

The look he gives me has me whimpering.

"You'll get what you want, Siren, but first I need to fully examine my present."

His head lowers and I cry out when he lowers one of the cups and sucks my nipple into his mouth. His other hand teases down my stomach and I pray it's heading to where I need it. He caresses the inside of my thigh for a bit and another whimper slips past my lips. Finally, his hand shifts and he teases my clit through the material of my thong. He hooks a finger in the material and my eyes widen.

He isn't... He wouldn't...

Luke yanks on the material, snapping it before tossing it somewhere in the room and I glare at him.

"Those were brand new and I really liked them."

He smirks. "I'll buy you more, but I know you aren't really be mad at me because your pussy is gushing even more than before."

I don't get a chance to respond because he shoves two fingers inside of me, which go in easily with how wet I am. I cry out as my body finally gets a little of what I needed. I claw at his shoulders as he starts to pump his fingers in and out of me.

"Give me your marks as you ride my fingers, Siren."

He goes back to teasing my breasts and nipples with his mouth and occasionally, he curls his fingers, hitting that bundle of nerves just right.

Right when I'm about to cum, his fingers leave me and when I glare at him, he chuckles. He fucking chuckles.

Flipping up my skirt a bit, he kisses down my thigh and I cry out again when he sucks my clit into his mouth before fucking me with his tongue. I grind against him, loving the feel of his beard against my thighs and against my pussy. He usually doesn't grow a beard because of his job at the hospital. While they do have beard nets, he doesn't like wearing them. However, when he has a long vacation, he usually lets it grow out since he knows how much I like it.

After a few moments, he goes back to teasing my clit and then his fingers are filling me up again, rubbing against that bundle of nerves. My hands grab onto his hair as I grind harder against him.

"Yes, yes, yes. So close."

Luke grazes my clit with his teeth and I cry out as my orgasm crests. My hands grasp for a pillow to cover my face with, but I can't find them. Luke quickly covers me, muffling my cry with a kiss as I ride his fingers through the rest of my orgasm, but I need more friction.

He must get the hint that I need more, because he lines up and enters me in one thrust.

"Yes, more, please give me more. Harder."

I'm not sure what's come over me, but thankfully Luke doesn't make me wait.

"Hang onto the headboard, Siren."

My core tightens at his order and he groans. Once my hands are in place, he pulls out, almost completely, before slamming back into me. He fucks me hard, just how I need it, but he also somehow makes it so his pelvis rubs my clit on each thrust. My orgasm slams into me out of nowhere.

I whimper when Luke suddenly pulls out, but judging by the look in his eyes, I know what he wants. I scramble to get on my hands and knees and he groans when I get into position.

"Fuck, Baby. I love your ass. It's so sexy in this dress."

His hand comes down hard on my ass, and I moan in response. I love getting spanked by Luke because it usually means what comes next will have me feeling his cock inside me for days after this.

"Your ass pinkens so beautifully for me." He rubs the sting away after another strike, and I'm damn near panting as I wait for him to fill me again.

"Please," I beg.

His hands grasp my hair and he pulls my head back slightly, kissing up my neck as he rubs his hard cock in between my ass cheeks.

"Please what, Siren?"

I whimper. "Please fuck me, Luke."

He bites down where my shoulder meets my neck as he finally pushes inside me and I don't even care that I'll probably have a hickey tomorrow that I'll need to try and cover up.

Moaning, I rock back, meeting his thrusts and loving how deep I can feel him.

"That's it, Baby. You take my cock so beautifully."

I cry out when I feel his hand come down hard again on my ass and I lean into the bed to muffle my cries as a few more slaps have tingles racing up my spine. He grabs my hips, and by limiting how much I can move, his thrusts seem to go even deeper.

My orgasm comes out of nowhere and Luke curses before I feel him cuming inside of me.

When he pulls out, he heads into the bathroom for a washcloth and I turn onto my side, panting and loving how tingly I'm feeling.

I hum in thanks when he cleans me up but then gasp when I see him. "How are you still hard?"

The corner of his lips tilts up into a sexy smirk. "I've been thinking about you all day, Siren. Think you're able to take me one more time?"

I bite my lip as my core clenches. He groans, having felt it as he cleans up his cum.

Tossing the washcloth somewhere, he leans over me again.

"This time, I'm taking my time and am going to tease the fuck out of you, Siren." He smirks as his fingers tease my ass, pulling a whimper from me. "Wouldn't want Santa to get mad at me for not inspecting my present properly."

Fuck, I think I need to get more dress-up outfits if this is how he's going to respond to them.

Chapter 10
Mary

THE NEXT MORNING, THE sound of a pained grunt wakes me up and I smile as I blink awake, already knowing what probably happened.

Looking over my shoulder, I see that it's 6 am. Again. Turning back toward them, I'm not surprised to see Cassie sitting on Luke's stomach. Thankfully, we'd changed into our Christmas pajamas after our last round of love making last night. Luke found the new toys I'd gotten and teased me for what felt like forever before he made love to me, nice and slow.

"Daddy! Μαμά (Mom)! You aren't going to believe it, but Santa came just like he said he would, and he left *a lot* of presents under the Christmas tree!"

I bite my lip and squeeze my thighs together at the look that passes over his face as he watches her excitedly talk about the presents. Fuck, this man just slays me with how much he loves the kids. It makes me want to have another baby with him. Or maybe more than one. We aren't doing anything to prevent a pregnancy, so fingers crossed, it will happen soon.

"Why don't you head out to the living room, ἄγγελε (angel)? Μαμά (Mom) and I will be out in a few minutes. Then we can open presents, okay?"

"Yesssss!" she yells as she climbs down off of Luke and crawls out of bed, yelling to her brothers the plan.

I smile and can't help the laugh that bubbles out of me as I turn back toward Luke. "Guess we better get ready."

He leans in, kissing me. "Guess so. I don't think they'll wait much longer so how about you take this bathroom. I'll get the coffee started and use the other bathroom."

"Sounds like a plan."

Carefully, I scoot to the edge of the bed, loving how I can still feel Luke from last night, and grab my scooter. I cannot thank Doc enough for getting this for me. It's given me back so much more of my mobility than the chair did. Not that we'll ever get rid of the chair. In fact, it's in the basement of the clubhouse in case someone ever needs to use it again.

I quickly do my business, brush my teeth and brush my hair, pulling it up into a bun on the top of my head. Since I'm sure there will be pictures, I head back into the bedroom, slip off my top and put on a bra. I do not want to be nipping out in any of the pictures, as I'm sure there will be a lot with this being our first Christmas together. Slipping my shirt back on, I make sure I didn't mess up my bun and then head out into the kitchen. I sigh in relief when I smell the sweet aroma of the coffee being brewed. Knowing Luke will get me a mug when it's ready, I head over to the living room and pause.

Cassie wasn't kidding. There are a ton more presents that Luke added to the pile after I headed into our room last night. My head whips to him in surprise and he gives me a sheepish smile from the kitchen as he fills our mugs and brings them into the living room. However, I can't find it in me to be mad at him for this. It's a good thing the kids' rooms are big because I think we'll need to order a few more bookcases or maybe even toy bins. Looking at the pile again I nod. Maybe both.

"To make this easier, how about we sort the presents? You each can claim a spot where you can put your presents. Then, once everything's sorted, we can open them up."

It takes a while with how many presents there are, but soon, everyone's got their presents in a pile near them.

"Okay, kiddos. Let 'er rip."

I snort at Luke's words, but it has the desired effect as all three kids rip into their presents.

I end up taking way too many pictures, and I'm sure Luke has a ton as well. Looking down at my presents, I smile. I have some new jewelry; some blank recipe books and supplies that I can't wait to use—I plan to use some of them for preparing recipes for the restaurant; a couple of new aprons and one of them has the name *Family Roots* on it, which will be the name of my restaurant; a Kindle e-reader; a fair number of paperback books; and a couple of sets of new kitchen knives, the good ones, which I absolutely can't wait to try out.

Luke got a couple of leather jackets—one that's heavier for winter and a lighter one for when it's warmer out; a pair of riding gloves; a switchblade; the watch he'd been wanting since his last one died not too long ago; and a few shirts that the kids had custom ordered for him stating he's the best dad ever. He'd quickly proclaimed that as soon as they were washed, he'd wear one of them.

The kids got tons of toys, books, video games, multiple brick building sets, clothes, shoes, and movies. Luke even got them all leather jackets which made me worried because they're all still growing like weeds, but when they tried them on, I was relieved that they were a little big. Hopefully they'll still fit come spring.

As we clear away the last of the wrapping paper, Luke clears his throat. "What's that on the tree?"

I turn toward the tree, confused, and finally spot what he's talking about. Ash walks over to it and takes the envelope, opens it, and pulls out a card.

His little forehead creases in confusion. "It says Santa left something in the garage."

Cassie immediately shrieks and makes a beeline to the garage. She, well all the kids actually, have been in heaven today at all the presents. I cock my eyebrow in question at Luke but I don't have to wait long to find out what he'd gotten them.

"Μαμά (Mom)! Santa got us bikes!" Cassie shouts from the garage.

"And something that's like a 4-wheeler for all of us!" Izzy cries.

My eyes widen in surprise because those aren't cheap.

"Actually, it's a UTV so we can all go out together," Luke whispers in my ear and I whip my head around to stare at him. That had to have cost almost damn near as much as a car!

Luke's cheeks pinken and he dips his head slightly. "Mary, other than the mortgage for your house and buying my bike and truck, I didn't have a lot of expenses, so I saved up a lot of the years."

He tugs me forward, but I'm still a bit irked. I know we'll have my trust fund to help with costs going forward, both for our home and for the restaurant, but I still kind of wish he would have talked to me first before getting us something so expensive.

"Baby, think of it as an investment and something that we'll have for years to come. When it's nicer, we'll go out on the trails and have some fun."

My body stiffens upon mention of the trails and memories threaten to bombard me from when Stephan and Derrick tried to kidnap me.

"That was part of my plan," Luke says softly. "The trails are gorgeous and I wanted to try and replace those memories. Plus, if you know the woods around here better, that should help for if there's ever trouble in the future."

Sighing, I finally nod. He's got a point, on both accounts. I want to erase what I can about Stephan from my mind, and honestly, heading out on the trails does sound fun.

"Okay, but next time, please talk to me before making such a big purchase."

He leans forward, kissing me. "Deal." He smiles and tugs on my hand before reaching out with his other arm and grabbing my scooter. "Now, how about we go and see what Santa brought?" he says with a wink which has me smiling despite still being sort of irked.

I still can't believe I got so lucky as to find Luke again after all these years. Yeah, the kids and I had to go through hell to get here, but I still wouldn't change a thing.

Leaning against the door frame, I smile as the kids ride their bicycles around the garage. Apparently sometime last night, Luke must have moved both of our cars out of the garage because both stalls are empty. Well, minus the space the UTV is currently taking up. But Luke didn't just get the kids bicycles, he also got them little motorized motorcycles like Jordan's.

Though, we need to wait for the kids to learn how to use those. One because another storm is coming in later today that will drop a few inches of snow on us, and two, they need to master riding a bicycle first. All three of their bicycles have training wheels on them because they'd never ridden one before. They're all motivated to learn because of Luke's rule that they can't ride their motorcycles until they can ride their bikes without training wheels.

I hear something vibrate and pat around for my phone, frowning when I realize I don't have it. Crap! What time is it? I look over to Luke as he stands and digs his phone out of his pocket and smiles.

"Levi just texted that breakfast is almost ready. How about we get dressed and head up to the clubhouse?"

I grin and shake my head, smiling, but I clap my hands a couple of times to cut through the kids' groaning and complaining. "Run upstairs and change, kiddos. After breakfast you'll be able to play some more." They grumble slightly but do as I ask.

Pivoting my scooter, I head into our room and into the bathroom. Hastily, I strip and wrap my cast as I prepare to take an insanely fast shower.

Twenty minutes later, Luke pulls our SUV up to the clubhouse. The kids still have no idea what's to come, and it's becoming harder to contain my smile.

Ash gets my scooter out of the back seat and Luke carries me up the porch steps. They must have been watching because Sasha opens the door for us.

As soon as the kids enter the clubhouse, they freeze at the sight of all the presents under the tree.

"More presents?" Izzy asks, his voice barely above a whisper.

"Yup, next is the club Christmas. But breakfast first, kiddo," Sasha replies as she ruffles his hair.

The three of us laugh as they make a beeline for the pass-through window.

"Maybe I should have specified when *all* of us are done with breakfast," she mutters and both Luke and I nod in agreement.

We follow the kids and I'm relieved when I see it's a pretty simple breakfast today with pancakes, eggs, bacon, and some fruit. Most of the club is out here already and it looks like they've recently gone through the line since their plates are still piled high. Luke helps Cassie and Izzy get their plates while I help Ash get his as well as mine.

Minutes later, we're all settled around one of the tables as we dig into our breakfasts. Timber, Mae, Levi, Thor & Dragon are sitting near us and are grinning as the kids excitedly tell them what all they got for Christmas. None of them are surprised, so I'm guessing they knew Luke had planned to go a bit overboard.

"I'll have to come over to check out your UTV. I was thinking of getting something for us to go out on the trails too," Thor says and Timber nods in agreement.

"Same. I mean we have the couple that belong to the club, but I'd like one for us as well."

"Sounds like a trend is starting," Levi says with a wink and I shake my head as I laugh. Trend indeed.

"**Μαμά** (Mom), can we open presents now?" Cassie asks me and I raise an eyebrow in question at Levi since she spearheaded this.

"We need to wait a few more minutes, Angel, before we can get started. We're waiting on Nikki and Sadie as well as Axe, Susie, and Jordan to arrive. They just left their houses to head here so it won't be long before they get here. After they've had breakfast, then we'll be able to open presents."

We chat for a few more minutes and when the doors open revealing Nikki, Axe, Susie, and the kids. Like our kids, Sadie and Jordan are excited for more presents and almost run to the food line to get their breakfasts.

About twenty minutes later, a whistle rings through the air and I turn, seeing Levi and Thor standing up in front of the Christmas tree. Levi claps her hands as she looks around.

"Alright, first and foremost, I hope everyone has had a Merry Christmas so far!" Levi pauses as the kids cheer, smiling at them. "We've got some more presents to hand out, but I think we need some helpers. Any volunteers?"

I don't think there's a face in the room that isn't smiling when all of the kids run forward, even Ash who I thought we'd have to encourage to participate.

"Okay, kiddos, before you help us out, we have a little something for you," Levi tells them and Thor opens the box that's on a nearby table and starts handing out little Santa hats that have the club's logo and each kid's name stitched into them.

Then, they start handing out presents and stockings to everyone. For the adults, we decided to do Secret Santa's. We all put our names into a bucket that had a couple of gift ideas jotted down on it—one bucket for the guys and one for the girls. Though, it was specified that the gifts weren't limited to just those items on the lists. However, the stockings are all gifts from the club I heard.

After a few minutes, we each have our presents and stockings and Thor gives the okay to open them up.

I darn near squeal in excitement when I see a basket containing a variety of bath bombs and a couple scents of moisturizer. "Oh my god, I can't wait to properly soak in a tub once I get this blasted cast off!" I exclaim happily.

Luke chuckles next to me. "Well, fingers crossed, that will happen in a couple of weeks."

I do a little happy dance in my chair. I can't wait!

Luke got a new hunting knife that he'd been wanting and I open my mouth to say how gorgeous the handle is when an excited shout has me looking around the room.

Timber raises his head, looking around the room. "I'm just gonna start this off. Dragon?"

Dragon laughs and nods. "I got his information from Levi. Glad you like it."

My gaze bounces between Timber and Dragon in confusion but Luke smiles, shaking his head slightly. "I'm going to take a stab, no pun intended, that Timber got a knife made by Gray Miller."

I frown. Where have I heard that name before?

"Gray makes all of Levi's, Sasha's, and Alexei's knives."

"Ah, thank you, I was trying to figure out where I heard that name before. He used to throw knives with Levi, right?"

He nods and goes to say something else when Thor whistles to grab everyone's attention. As we go around the room saying who had who for the Secret Santa, I snuggle deeper into Luke's side. He really did deliver on his promise to give us the best Christmas.

In fact, I'd say it's a damn near perfect Christmas.

And like Luke said before, it's a Christmas that I'm almost positive we'll all remember.

A Biker's Prayer

May the sun rise in front of me,
the rain fall behind me
and the wind follow me.
May the angels guard my travels
for they know what is ahead of me.
Keep me safe through
rolling hills and swirling turns.
Let the eagle guide me
to the mountain tops.
Let the moon's light
guide me through the night.
Lord, thank you for letting me be a biker.

Author's Note

THANK YOU EVERYONE FOR reading *Steel Archangel's MC: A SAMC Christmas to Remember (SAFC3.5)!*

I hope you enjoyed the club's first Christmas story!

Next up in the series is Reaper's story as he helps his Darlin' heal after a traumatic injury and works to claim his woman, his Neith, his hunter that owns his heart <3 However, before he can do all that, he has to overcome his own demons. Can Reaper and his Neith save each other?

Reviews are very important for authors, and especially to new authors! Thank you to everyone that leaves a review, even if it is only a line or two or just leaving stars! Keep reading for info on how to contact me as well as other books by me. I'd love to hear from you!

About the Author

R. KNIGHT LOVES READING and writing romance novels, whether it be contemporary, MC, paranormal, reverse harem or menage. If you like strong women and partners surrounded by the men who adore and worship them, then follow me to hear about current and upcoming books that will satisfy your craving!

When R. Knight isn't reading or writing, she's spending time with her amazing husband, two kiddos, and two cats where they live in Eastern Wisconsin. The usual shenanigans involve watching movies, camping, playing board games and/or video games.

https://linktr.ee/Author_R_Knight